Why Don't the Stars Fall Down?

Especially for my sister, Peggy Ribbons,
and for Bethan and James Parker

Why Don't the Stars Fall Down?

Jan Godfrey
Illustrated by D'reen Neeves

Augsburg
MINNEAPOLIS

Billy Bear and Bessie Bear went to stay
with Auntie Bear and Uncle Bear.

At bedtime they played camping.
Auntie Bear put them both to bed in a tent in the garden.
It was fun going to bed outside.
They could smell the flowers and the grass.
They could hear the birds going to sleep in the trees.
They could just see a hedgehog creeping across the lawn.

Billy Bear and Bessie Bear looked out of the tent.
Lots of stars shone in the dark night sky.
The stars looked extra bright tonight.
They were shining and twinkling and sparkling.

"Why don't the stars fall down?" Billy Bear asked Bessie.

"I don't know," said Bessie Bear.

"But if they did I could decorate my sleeping bag with them."

"Why don't the stars fall down?" Billy Bear asked Auntie Bear.
"I don't know," said Auntie Bear.
"But they sparkle like my best necklace.
It's time to go to sleep now, Billy Bear and Bessie Bear.
Goodnight."

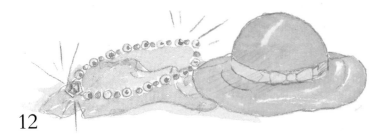

Bessie Bear went to sleep.

Billy Bear pretended to go to sleep.

But he heard Night-Time Owl hooting outside.

He peeped out of the tent again.

He looked up at the stars in the night sky.

He crept out on to the grass.

"Why don't the stars fall down?" Billy Bear asked Owl.
"Are they stuck on the sky with glue?"
"I shouldn't think so," said Owl.
"There wouldn't be enough glue for all the sky.
Why don't you ask Bat? He's hanging around somewhere."

"Why don't the stars fall down?" Billy Bear asked Bat.
"Do they hold on upside down – like you do?"
"I don't know," said Bat. "And anyway, I must fly.
Why don't you ask Cat? She's got sharp eyes. She'll know."
And Bat flitted away into the night.

Just then Cat came along.

Billy Bear could see her green eyes gleaming.

"Why don't the stars fall down?" asked Billy Bear.

"Are they stitched on like buttons?"

"I don't know anything about buttons," said Cat.

"All I know about is catching mice.

Good night, Billy Bear."

So Billy Bear went back into the tent
and snuggled down in his sleeping bag.
Billy Bear tried to sleep.
But he went on wondering.
Why don't the stars fall down?
If one fell, would it hit Bessie Bear on the nose?
That made him giggle!

Billy Bear giggled and giggled so much
that Uncle Bear came out into the garden.
"What's the matter, Billy Bear?" asked Uncle Bear.
"Why don't the stars fall down?" asked Billy Bear.

Uncle Bear sat down on Billy's sleeping bag and said:
"God has put the stars in the sky.
They're like tiny suns far away in space.
They can't fall down because they are moving away from us.
But they're so far, far, far away that you can't see them moving."

Then Uncle Bear let Billy Bear look through his telescope.
Billy Bear could see lots and lots of stars twinkling and shining.
They were so beautiful he wanted to look at them all night long.

"I'm glad God keeps all the stars in the sky," yawned Billy Bear. And he curled up in his sleeping bag and fell asleep.

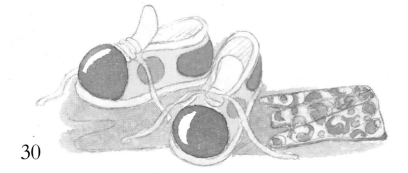

WHY DON'T THE STARS FALL DOWN?

First North American edition published 1994 by Augsburg Books
First published by Tamarind Books, in association with SU Publishing,
London, England

Copyright © 1993 AD Publishing Services Ltd
Text copyright © 1993 Jan Godfrey
Illustrations copyright © 1993 D'reen Neeves

ISBN 0-8066-2743-3   LCCN 94-070318

Manufactured in Singapore   AF 9-2743

98   97   96   95   94   1   2   3   4   5   6   7   8   9   10